THE ISLAND OF ANIMALS

DENYS JOHNSON-DAVIES

ILLUSTRATED BY SABIHA KHEMIR

QUARTET BOOKS

For Frances

First published by Quartet Books Limited 1994
A member of the Namara Group
27 Goodge Street
London W1P 1FD

Text copyright © by Denys Johnson-Davies 1994
Illustrations copyright © by Sabiha Khemir 1994

British Library Cataloguing in Publication Data

Johnson-Davies, Denys
Island of Animals
I. Title II. Khemir, Sabiha
823.914 [F]

ISBN 0 7043 7016 6

Printed and bound in Great Britain

CONTENTS

PREFACE

The *Epistles of the Brethren of Purity*, of which 'The Dispute between Animals and Man' was one, were compiled in Basra during the tenth century AD. Scholars have held various views about the identity and political and intellectual affiliations of the individuals who made up the group of philosophers and theologians responsible for writing the *Epistles*, but all agree they are among the masterpieces of classical Arabic literature.

'The Dispute between Animals and Man' is the most well known of the *Epistles* and must rank high among the world's animal fables, being unique for the manner in which it argues the case for animal rights. In adapting it for the English reader, I have shortened it considerably, though I have lengthened both the first and final chapters.

INTRODUCTION

Written in Basra in the fourth century of the Islamic era (tenth century AD), the text from which the present book has been adapted expresses in the form of a fable the teachings of Islam about man's responsibilities towards animals. It asks the question: In what respect, if any, is man superior to animals, and by virtue of what qualities is he entitled to think that he has unaccountable mastery over the members of the animal kingdom? The answer in Islamic terms must be surprising for any reader for whom God Himself has been largely relegated to the realm of fantasy. For the Muslim, the answer is both natural and inevitable: quite simply, man in the final resort is distinguished from animals not necessarily by any intellectual or moral superiority but by the fact that he has been chosen — for good or bad — to be the sole creature answerable at his death for his actions and who has been promised an afterlife whose nature will depend on how he has conducted himself in this world.

In Arabia in pre-Islamic times — in the 'Jahiliyya' or 'Time of Ignorance' — animals were accorded no consideration and were simply there to be exploited by man. With the coming of Islam and its Prophet, man's attitude towards himself and the nature that surrounds him was radically changed: through its teachings he was shown that he was merely part of a cohesive whole. The Qur'an, which together with the Traditions (the Sayings of the Prophet) provides the basic teachings of Islam, has five of its chapters named after animals and makes mention of many more. Numerous verses deal with the place of animals in God's creation and no verse is more fundamental on the subject than the words: 'And there is no animal in the earth nor bird that flies with its two wings, but that they are communities like yourselves'.[1] The Qur'an states why it is that man has been made responsible for animals — and indeed for the whole of God's creation. The Qur'an tells man: 'And He has appointed you as regents in the earth.'[2] Thus man has been created by God to share the bounties of the earth with all the other creatures that inhabit it — 'And the earth He has assigned to all living creatures.'[3] Many references are also made to the fact that animals have been created for man's benefit — 'It is God who provided you all manner of livestock, that you may ride on some of them and from some of them you may derive your food. And there are other uses in them to satisfy your heart's desires.

It is on them, as in ships, that you make your journeys.'[4] While they have been created for man's benefit, their safekeeping has been entrusted to him — as has the safekeeping of the world as a whole. A well-known Tradition of the Prophet says: 'The world is green and beautiful

and God has appointed you as His stewards over it.' In another, man is enjoined that if he has a palm-shoot in his hand at the moment when the world is about to come to an end he should nevertheless plant it.[5]

In Islam no animal should be killed — with certain exceptions such as snakes and scorpions — unless for food.[6] When slaughtering animals every care should be taken to see that the animal suffers as little as possible. Prophetic Traditions exist enjoining that the knife be well sharpened, that animals should not be kept waiting and that they should not be able to witness other animals being slaughtered. An interesting extension of this is mentioned in a book about Jewish travellers to the Arab world in the Middle Ages where instructions are given as to the general behaviour they should observe so as not to offend against Muslim manners and customs. 'It is also their custom,' says Rabbi Meshullam Ben R. Menahem of Volterra on a journey undertaken in 1481, 'to give no fodder to donkeys and nothing to drink, only all the caravan together, for it is by their law a great sin that the other horses or small donkeys should see one of them eat, because that would hurt those that are not eating, and that is cruelty to animals.'[7] Thus a Tradition records that the Prophet, seeing a man sharpening his blade as the animal waited, reprimanded him with the words: 'Do you wish to slaughter the animal twice: once by sharpening your blade in front of it and another time by cutting its throat?'[8]

Through the numerous Prophetic Traditions about animals runs the Messenger of God's concern for their welfare; many of them state that man will be rewarded for all acts of kindness performed for the sake of animals in the same way as acts of kindness to his fellow men will be recorded in his favour. One of the best known is the Tradition that tells of a man who was walking along a road and felt thirsty. Finding a well, he lowered himself into it and drank. When he came out he found a dog painting from thirst and licking at the earth. He therefore went down again into the well and filled his shoe with water and gave it to the dog. For this act God Almighty forgave him his sins. The Prophet was then asked whether man had a reward through animals, and he replied: 'In everything that lives there is a reward.'[9]

Similar stories are to be found in the extensive literature written about the Sufis, the mystics of Islam. One such is recounted in al-Damiri's book *The Life of Animals*[10] in which one of the friends of the great Sufi al-Shibli tells of seeing him in a dream after he had died. He asked him what God had done with him, to which al-Shibli replied that God had placed him before Him and asked him if he knew why He had forgiven him his sins. Al-Shibli had suggested that it might be because of the good works he had done, the prayers he had performed, his fastings and pilgrimages, his having associated with pious people and his journeyings in search of knowledge. To all this God replied that these were not the reason. Al-Shibli had answered that these were the only things he could think of that might have saved him, to which God had said: 'Do you remember when you were walking in the lanes of Baghdad and you found a small cat made weak by the cold creeping from wall to wall because of the great cold and ice, and out of pity you took it and put it inside a fur you were wearing so as to protect it from the pains of the cold? Because of the mercy you showed that cat I have had mercy on you.'

While concerned about the kind treatment of all animals, the Prophet was known to have a particular affection for cats. An unauthenticated and possibly apocryphal — though none the less charming — story tells of how he was once talking with some of his Companions when

a cat came and seated itself on his cloak. When he wished to rise to his feet he cut out the piece of the cloak on which the cat was sleeping so as not to disturb it. While in Islam the dog is regarded as unclean and direct contact with it requires that a person must redo his ablutions for prayer, the cat makes no such demands. The Prophet's wife 'A'ishah reported how he once put down some water for a cat and then made his ablutions in what remained after the cat had drunk its fill. Another Tradition tells of how the Prophet was invited to a man's house and accepted, but he was then invited to another house and declined the invitation. Asked about this, he answered, 'In so-and-so's house there is a dog.' When told that in the other man's house there was a cat, the Messenger of God replied that cats were not unclean but were like the servants who come and go in one's home.[11] Al-Damiri gives an amusing account of how, traditionally, the cat came into being. When Noah collected up all the animals in pairs in the Ark, the people who were there complained that the mice were polluting their food, so God made the lion give a sneeze and the cat — the traditional enemy of mice — was brought into being.[12]

On the question of Islam's general attitude to dogs, a modern writer[13] has suggested as a main reason for it the fear of rabies, a disease that was widespread in the Arab world. Arabic literature, nevertheless, contains numerous instances in which such characteristics of dogs as intelligence and loyalty to man are lauded.[14] Many of the stories show that dogs no less than cats and other animals were the recipients of acts of kindness from men. They also show that the incentive towards treating animals well had its roots in a strongly based religious tradition. One such story tells of the Imam Ahmad who, learning of a man who might be in a position to tell him about Prophetic Traditions, sets off to meet him. On arriving he finds that the man is feeding his dog and makes the Imam wait till he has finished. The Imam Ahmad is annoyed at this and asks the man how it is that he appears to show preference for his dog over the visitor. The man admits to this and in his reply mentions a Tradition of the Prophet: '"He who dashes the hope of someone who has expected something from him, God will dash his hope on the Day of Judgement, and he will not enter Paradise." This dog sought me out and I fear to dash its hope lest God dashes my hope in Him.'

Stories were also told by the Prophet about people who are punished by God for their ill-treatment of animals. Every Muslim knows the story[15] of the woman who was condemned to Hell-fire because of a cat she had imprisoned, giving it neither food nor water and not allowing it to find its own food. This Tradition illustrates the essential Muslim attitude towards animals whereby man should as far as possible allow them to live out their lives in a natural manner; here the woman had sinned not only because she did not feed the cat but because she had not allowed it to be free to fend for itself. Thus the jurisprudents of Islam held that it is up to the owner of an animal to provide for it the necessities of life; if he is unable to do so, then he should sell it, let it go free in some place where it can find shelter and food, or — if it is an animal that can be legally eaten — he should slaughter it. They even suggested that such responsibilities extended beyond the owner of the animal himself, so that were a blind cat to take refuge in someone's house he would become automatically responsible for it. So, too, the keeping of birds in cages is against the precepts of Islam, and the story is told of one of the Companions of the Prophet who used to buy, and then set free, sparrows that had been caught by young boys.

To kill or harm animals by way of sport is wholly reprehensible. Thus the Prophet is reported as having said: 'He who kills a sparrow uselessly, it cries out to God on the Day of Resurrection and says: "O Lord, Your servant killed me uselessly and not for any benefit."'[16] Whereas here and elsewhere animals are shown as being able to complain to the Almighty about their treatment at the hands of men on earth, the general consensus in Islam is that animals will not enjoy any form of afterlife, which is the view expressed in the present book. None the less there have been schools of thought that have put forward a more positive view on behalf of animals.[17]

All forms of blood sport, where the aim is enjoyment rather than the procuring of food, were forbidden in Islam. It was thus specifically prohibited to tie up animals for the purpose of making targets of them. Inciting animals to fight one another was also forbidden by the Prophet; such sports as bear-baiting and cock-fighting, which thrived in Europe, were unknown in the Arab world. Ever-practical in his teachings, the Prophet declared that the meat of animals killed in such a way was unlawful and could not be eaten. Various pre-Islamic practices such as cutting off the humps of camels and the tails of sheep — these humps and tails were then available for food without the necessity of slaughtering the animals themselves — were the subject of interdiction, and here again the Prophet declared such meat unlawful.

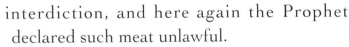

Special treatment was naturally given to riding animals and beasts of burden, animals which played an essential part in the life of

early Islam. There are many injunctions against overloading them or branding them on their faces, or riding them for too long periods or without adequate food and water. For instance, the Prophet, seeing a man seated on his camel and addressing people in the market-place, said: 'Do not take the backs of your riding animals as thrones.'[18] On another occasion he saw a camel so emaciated that its stomach was touching its back and he said: 'Have a fear of God where these dumb animals are concerned.'[19] A close Companion of the Prophet reported that when travelling with him they never performed their prayers before they had unburdened their animals.[20] The Prophet also recommended that when journeying through an area full of vegetation one should go slowly and allow the riding animals to graze, but that one should hurry through arid terrain.[21]

In his essay 'On Cruelty', the sixteenth-century writer Montaigne, before his time in many respects, remarks that, 'Natures that are bloodthirsty towards animals show a native propensity towards cruelty.' This brings to mind the story that has been recorded of a man who had been summoned by the Caliph so that he might appoint him as a judge. The Caliph, looking down from an upstairs room, sees the man striking his horse as he tethers it and changes his mind about appointing him. How can a man who treats an animal in such a way be given powers of judgement over men?

Bull-fighting, too, would have incurred the Prophet's disapproval. Recently, following the disastrous fall in tourism that resulted from the Gulf War, a suggestion was made in Egypt that tourism might be boosted by the introduction of bull-fighting. This suggestion was hotly rejected in one of the papers by an assurance that such spectacles, so abhorrent to Islam, would never be countenanced in a Muslim country. A typical Muslim view about such sports was given by a Moroccan ambassador to the Court of Spain who was invited to a bull-fight. 'When we were asked about it,' he reported, 'we replied perforce, out of courtesy, that we had liked their games, but we really believed the exact opposite, for the torture of animals is not permitted by the law of God or by the law of nature.'[22] This, however, is not to say that animals are not ill-treated in the Muslim world. Sadly, in this and other respects, Islam's teachings are often not observed. None the less the belief that man will be answerable in the Hereafter for his ill-treatment of animals still prevails in Islam. In the district of Cairo in which I live I recently saw a small desert fox for sale housed in a diminutive cage in a pet shop. I talked to a neighbouring grocer about this and he informed me that he had remonstrated with the owner of the shop to no avail. 'But,' he added, 'he will be accountable to the Almighty.' On the whole, such cruelty as exists results from ignorance and poverty; there are few instances of gratuitous cruelty as are sometimes practised in the West. It is interesting to note that the Arabist Edward Lane, writing in the early years of the last century, observed: 'In my earlier intercourse with the people of Egypt, I was much pleased at observing their humanity to dumb animals; to see a person who gathered together the folds of his loose clothes to prevent their coming in contact with a dog, throw to the impure animal a portion of the bread which he was eating . . .' He then remarks that in the meantime the generality of Egyptians has changed in this respect for the worse, and he continues: '. . . but I am inclined to think that the conduct of Europeans has greatly conduced to produce this effect, for I do not remember to have seen acts of cruelty to dumb animals except in places where Franks either reside or are frequent visitors — as Alexandria, Cairo, and Thebes.'[23]

Historical documents from the Middle Ages refer to gifts being made by individuals for the welfare of animals. Montaigne, in this same essay 'On Cruelty', talks of the Turks, i.e., the Muslims, having almshouses and hospitals for animals. Today, in some of the magnificent mosques of Istanbul, one can see, built into the outer structure, shelters for birds made in small mosque-like replicas. On the mausoleum of the Imam al-Shafi'i, built in Cairo in 1211, there is a small metal trough built in the shape of a boat made for the purpose of holding grain for birds.

In the West, following the pattern of ancient Greece and Rome, not only were animals regarded as expendable and subjected to such horrors as 'the Games' in Rome, but they were also made the subject of such grotesque and farcical happenings as being put on trial for so-called offences and subsequently sentenced and punished — as for instance cats being burnt alive for consorting with witches. Any student of Roman law will know of how an ox, guilty of goring a man to death, had itself to be put to death, not because it might kill others but as a punishment for its wrongdoing. Another gratuitous cruelty practised in Europe in the Middle Ages was to make a dog suffer death by hanging it with a condemned man in order to highlight the heinous nature of his crime. In Islam, on the other hand, animals have never been held to share with humans an ability to distinguish between right and wrong, and cannot therefore be made accountable for their actions.

Just as it is not permissible to kill animals for one's enjoyment, so too the Prophet prohibited the use of the skins of beasts of prey as floor coverings,[24] and, in another Tradition, of leopard skins as saddle-covers.[25] These interdictions may have resulted from his natural dislike of ostentation or from the fact that beasts of prey, which cannot be eaten, would be likely to be killed solely for their skins. The skins of domesticated animals that have been slaughtered for food can, of course, be used for all such purposes.

The Prophet's injunctions regarding the treatment of animals were not restricted to physical cruelty: he was aware that they too possessed other feelings that should not be ignored. He thus once scolded his wife 'A'ishah for pulling too harshly on her camel when it was proving difficult to handle. 'You must be gentle,' he told her.[26] He also forbade the cutting of a horse's forelock, 'Because in it is the horse's seemliness or decorum,' or of its mane 'because it protects the horse', or of its tail 'because it is its fly-whisk'.[27] It was reported that some people were journeying with the Prophet when they came across a bird with two chicks. One of the men took the chicks and the mother bird came fluttering around them. When the Prophet saw this he asked: 'Who has caused this bird distress by taking her children? Return them to her.'[28]

In Islam one's duties to one's neighbours are of great importance — hence the Arabic proverb, 'Choose your neighbour before you choose your house.' Once a Companion of the Prophet, 'Adiyy ibn Hatim, was seen crumbling up bread for some ants with the words: 'They are our neighbours and have rights over us.'[29] On another occasion the well-known Imam Ishaq al-Shirazi was walking with a friend when a dog appeared on the road. The friend drove it away and the Imam said to him: 'Do you not know that the road is to be shared between it and us?'

Incorporated into Islam is the knowledge that man will be judged by his actions towards all of God's creatures and that

he risks incurring His wrath if he violates the trust placed in his hands as the Almighty's representative on earth. The ruler no less than his subjects was required to abide by these teachings, and the best of them did so. His sense of his overall responsibility towards his Maker was succinctly expressed in the words of the great Caliph Omar: 'Not a mule stumbles in Iraq without Omar being answerable.'

The stories and Prophetic Traditions recounted here are only a small part of those available on the subject of animals. Even if some are regarded as apocryphal, they exemplify an attitude founded not upon any humanistic philosophy or natural feelings of the heart but upon the basic teachings of a religion that came into being fourteen centuries ago. As such they show a very real understanding of man's proper attitude to his fellow creatures — a concern that has only recently begun to trouble the conscience of the West.

NOTES

1.   Qur'an 6.38
2.   Qur'an 25.39
3.   Qur'an 55.10
4.   Qur'an 40.79
5.   The collection of Imam Ahmad
6.   And in the case of harmful animals they should be despatched quickly and in no way tortured
7.   *Jewish Travellers* edited by Elkan Nathan Adler and published by George Routledge & Sons Ltd, 1930
8.   *Al-Furu' min al-Kafi* by al-Kilani
9.   To be found in the collections made by Muslim and by al-Bukhari, also in those of Malik, Imam Ahmad and Abu Da'ud
10.   *Hayat al-Hayawan al-Kubra* by Kamal al-Din al-Damiri
11.   In the collection of Imam Ahmad, also in those of al-Daraqutni, al-Hakim and al-Bayhaqi
12.   This story is recounted in Letter 18 of Montesquieu's *Lettres Persanes*
13.   *Dalil al-Muslim al-Hazin* by Husayn Ahmad Amin, Maktabat Madbuli, Cairo 1984
14   See, 'Tafdil al-kilab 'ala kathirin mimman labisa al-thiyab' ('Rating dogs as superior to many of those who wear clothes') by the tenth-century writer Abu Bakr Muhammad ibn Khalif ibn al-Marzaban — an anthology of prose and poetry in praise of the dog. Dar al-Tadamun, Beirut, 1992
15.   In the Sahih of Muslim
16.   In the collections of al-Nasa'i and of Ibn Habban
17.   See al-Ghazali's *The Remembrance of Death and the Afterlife*, translated by T. Winter, esp. his note on p. 201, Islamic Texts Society, Cambridge, 1989
18.   In the collection of Abu Da'ud
19.   In the collection of Abu Da'ud
20.   In the collection of Abu Da'ud
21.   In the collection of Muslim
22.   *The Muslim Discovery of Europe* by Bernard Lewis, Weidenfeld & Nicolson, 1982, p. 274
23.   *Manners and Customs of the Modern Egyptians* by Edward William Lane, first published in 1836, East-West Publications 1978, p. 286
24.   In the collection of Abu Da'ud
25.   In the collection of Abu Da'ud
26.   In the collection of Muslim
27.   In the collection of Abu Da'ud
28.   In the collection of Muslim
29.   In the collection of Abu Da'ud

THE ISLAND OF ANIMALS

1

MEN ARRIVE ON

THE ISLAND OF ANIMALS

Long ago and far away a ship was battling against the waves in a stormy sea. The passengers and crew, standing on the deck, clinging to the masts or each other, saw with terror the high walls of water that threatened to swallow them up. Lightning streaked and thunder cracked all around them, and the ship was tossed about by the winds like a matchstick. The captain stood pale and helpless as he saw his ship no longer under his control. The passengers were moving their lips in prayer, for they saw that nothing but a miracle could save them from death at the bottom of the ocean.

Suddenly the miracle happened and the captain saw that his ship was being driven towards a long island that lay, like a green strip of friendly grass, in the middle of that boiling ocean. The captain turned his face towards the heavens and spread out his hands in thanks to the Almighty who had rescued them from certain destruction. The passengers and the crew all joined together in prayers of thanks, then gave shouts of joy as the ship came to rest in a little bay where it was protected from the stormy winds.

Taking it in turns in the rowing boat they had on board, everyone disembarked. It was a great relief

to be on solid earth after the fears and hardships they had suffered on the ship buffeted by storms. As they explored the island they were amazed to find how beautiful and fertile it was. Apart from its lovely sandy shore, it had good rich soil, springs of fresh water and flowing streams, green fields and rich pastures, and many kinds of trees and plants with fruits and flowers. They also noticed that it was full of all the kinds of animals they had ever seen in their own countries. But what astonished them most of all was that the animals seemed to be completely tame and to have no fear of them. When they had walked from one side of the island to the other, passing by woods and   meadows, mountains and valleys, waterfalls and lakes, they all realized an extraordinary thing about this island: there was no sign of a human being.

'Can you imagine — we are the first men to have stepped on this island,' said one of the men.

'That is why the animals aren't frightened,' said another of the men.

'This is their island,' said a third man.

'The Island of Animals!' said a fourth man. 'An island where the animals rule.'

Though they were all agreed that they had never seen a more beautiful island, many of the men on the ship yearned to be back in their own countries with their relatives and friends, where they could enjoy the luxuries of civilization. Others, though, were entranced by the possibilities this island gave them of building a new life.

Suddenly, one of the men said, 'I would like to live here.'

'What? And leave your present home?' answered a friend in astonishment.

'And why not?' replied the man. 'Is not Allah everywhere?'

Many of the other men agreed with him: that the Island of Animals would be a lovely place in which to settle and make their homes. No less than seventy men decided to stay on the island. These men came from different parts of the world and were from different religions; they included Muslims, Christians, Jews and others. They were also men of every sort of profession, trade and craft. Thus there were among them doctors and lawyers and builders and carpenters and shopkeepers and farmers and fishermen and bakers and tailors. Between them, the seventy men possessed all the skills necessary for a full and happy life.

5

The men who had decided to continue their journey by sea helped the sailors to repair the damage the ship had suffered from the storm. When everything had been put right and the ship was ready to put to sea again, the seventy men lined up on the shore and waved goodbye to their friends. They called out to the men on the deck of the ship and the men on the ship answered back to their friends on the sandy shore.

'May Allah keep you safe!'

'May Allah guide you to a life of happiness!'

'May Allah bring you home safely!'

'May Allah prosper you in your new life!'

And soon the ship was out of sight, sailing away from the little bay of the Island of Animals on a calm blue sea.

2

THE ANIMALS REBEL

I t was true: the men who were now making their home on the island were the very first human beings to have set foot on it. Up till this moment the animals had had it to themselves. The only other creatures with whom they shared it were some Djinn, those creatures who, though we never see them, live among us. In the Qur'an it is told that the Prophet Muhammad, on whom be the blessings and peace of Allah, preached to the Djinn in the same way as he preached to mankind; thus many Djinn, just like many people, have become Muslims and live in accordance with the laws of Allah and the teachings of His Prophet.

The various animals and the Djinn lived together peacefully, for the Djinn did not interfere in the lives of the animals and allowed them complete freedom. Now, with the coming of man, everything changed. The seventy men were soon busy building themselves houses and making preparations for the sort of comfortable lives they had enjoyed in

8

their previous homes. Surrounded by so many animals, they remembered how, in the countries in which they had lived before, they had been able to benefit from animals: how they had used their milk and meat for food, and their skins and wool for clothing, while some of the animals, like horses, mules and donkeys, they used for riding from one place to another, for transporting goods and for drawing carts, or for working in the fields with ploughs. They knew that, without the help of animals, life could never be truly full and happy. So it was not long before the men had captured a number of animals and were keeping them for their own use and making them work for them. And they began killing some of them so that they could cook and eat them. Occasionally some men would go out to hunt the wild animals who lived in the woods and forests, or would trap them so that they could have their meat for food and their skins for clothing; sometimes they even hunted animals just for the pleasure and excitement of chasing after them and killing them.

The animals quickly realized how changed their lives had become since the arrival of men on their island. They talked to each other and compared the peaceful freedom in which they had been living with the harsh and cruel way in which man was now treating them. No longer did the animals rule the island; no longer did they come and go as they pleased.

'Why should man keep us locked up all night, or tied with a rope, and then make us work from early sunrise till sunset?' the donkeys, horses and mules asked each other.

'And why,' asked the cows and sheep, 'should our milk be taken away from us every day rather than given to our children? Then, without warning, our masters hold us down on our sides and cut our throats so that they can cook our flesh and use our skins for covering their floors or for making their shoes.'

'And why,' asked all the animals, 'should man think he has the right to treat us badly and beat us just because

we don't do exactly as he wants, or don't work hard enough because we are too tired and need to rest? Who is man, this strange creature who considers himself so superior to us animals, who feels he has the right to own us as though we were nothing but his slaves?'

So some of the animals rebelled against their masters and refused to go on working for them. When this happened the men punished them with blows from sticks and whips and threatened not to give them any more food or to allow them to go out into the fields to graze. A few of the animals succeeded in escaping from their masters and fled to those parts of the island where the men could not follow them. Those animals which were still in their masters' power were beaten even harder when they tried to shirk their work, and at night they were securely bolted in their stables or pens, or were tied up with ropes and chains.

After a while the animals saw that there was nothing they could do against the harsh treatment they were receiving.

'Man is strong and understands how to control us,' said the animals, and they bowed their heads and once again obeyed the commands of their masters.

'But it is not fair!' shouted some of the bolder animals. 'Even if man kills us with his beatings we shall not put up with such treatment.'

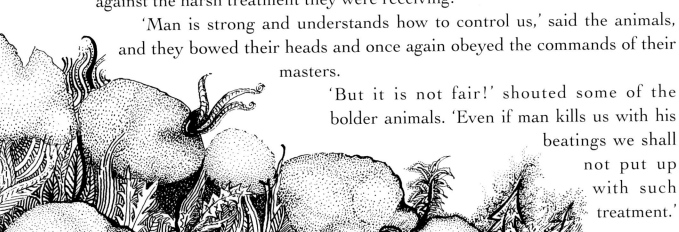

'How can we stop him from using us for his own benefit and being as cruel to us as he wants?' asked others, who wanted to rebel but were afraid of the beatings they would receive.

'It is unfair!' shouted all the farm animals, who had found that, with man's arrival on the island, they had become slaves.

They discussed among themselves whether there was anything they could do, but all agreed that they were helpless against man's superior intelligence and strength. Then one of them suggested that they should go and complain to the king of the Djinn and ask him to give judgement between the animals and man and to decide whether man had the right to behave in this manner. It was arranged that a mule, who had been left on his own out in a field, should act as their spokesman.

So the mule made his way secretly to the court of the king of the Djinn and reported to him that man was being cruel to the animals and treating them like slaves, and the mule asked him to be the judge between the animals and man.

3

THE KING OF THE DJINN

The king of the Djinn was both good and wise. He was a Muslim and all his subjects were followers of the teachings of Islam. Like a true Muslim he wanted nothing better than to please the Almighty and to see all His creatures living at peace with one another. On hearing from the mule about man's cruelty to the animals, he decided to look into the matter and so he sent a messenger to the men and asked them to come and visit him. When some of the men came to the king of the Djinn and heard that the animals were complaining against them, they were angry with the animals.

'But that's not right,' the men protested. 'After all, the animals are our slaves and we are their masters. Allah the Almighty has created the animals for man's benefit and yet some of them are now rebelling against us and refusing to do their work. Others have run away from the places we have made for them to live in. What, then, can we do to make them work but beat them? And what can we do to stop them escaping except to shut them in at night or tie them up?'

On hearing these words, the king of the Djinn thought deeply for a while,

then he spoke. 'You say, O men, that these animals are your slaves. Please give me proof of this.'

'This is a well-known fact, your majesty,' the men answered. 'Everyone knows this. Since time began the animals throughout the world have been under the command of man.'

'But give me proof,' repeated the king of the Djinn. 'It is not enough for you simply to say that this is well known. Tell me, if you can, how it was that it became accepted that animals were the slaves of man.'

'There are,' replied one of the men, 'many places in the Holy Books — in the Torah of the Jews, in the Gospels of the Christians and in the Qur'an of us Muslims — where it is clearly stated that the animals were created for the benefit of man.'

'Tell me of such a verse in the Holy Qur'an,' said the king of the Djinn.

'I shall quote, for instance,' replied the man, 'the verse where the Almighty said: "And He has created cattle for you from which you have clothing and many benefits and from which you eat."'

And the man then quoted other verses from the Holy Qur'an that talked about animals having been created for man's benefit, and the king of the Djinn listened with attention to what was said. Then the king of the Djinn asked the spokesman of the animals if he had anything to say in reply.

'It is true, your majesty,' said the mule, 'that in the same way as Allah created the heavens and the earth, and the sun and the moon and the clouds, He also created all the animals that live upon the earth's surface and in the seas. If, as man claims, we animals were created by Allah to help man, this does not mean that men are the masters and that we are nothing but their slaves. Man has no excuse for treating us in the cruel way he does. Where does he find any reason for thinking himself so superior to animals?'

At this one of the men rose to his feet and addressed the king of the Djinn. 'It must be obvious to everyone, from the way in which Allah has fashioned both animals and men, that the Almighty meant man to be the master of all animals. Do you not see, your majesty, that man was created to walk upright, with his head held proudly, while the animals were made to walk on four legs with their heads facing down towards the ground? Also, that man was created in proper and beautiful proportions, while animals are to be seen in all sorts of strange and misshapen forms? Look, for example, at the enormous body the camel has, what a long neck he has, but what small ears and what a tiny tail. The elephant, too, has a vast body, a long trunk, great tusks, very large ears and

small eyes. On the other hand, rabbits have a small body but very large ears. You can see, your majesty, how irregular are the bodies of animals in comparison with that of man.'

The mule, spokesman of the farm animals, considered the man's words, then replied, 'I do not agree at all with what the man has just said. First of all, man should know and recognize that all animals, like man himself, are the work of the wise Creator, who made them as they are for good reasons. It is clear, though, that men do not have the sense to see God's great wisdom in creating His various creatures as He has. Let us take as an example the camel: his long neck makes it possible for him to reach the ground where grow thegrasses and shrubs which are his food. As for the elephant, his powerful trunk makes it easy for him to tear off the leaves and branches from the trees, and by flapping his large ears he keeps the flies away from his face and eyes, while his powerful tusks have been given to him for defending himself against his enemies. And so too with the rabbit, who can use his large ears to provide him with warmth in winter and to protect him from the heat of the sun in summer. The Almighty, man should know, has fashioned all His creatures, large and small, in accordance with their particular needs, and it is not right for any one of His animals, man included, to claim that one animal is more beautifully formed than another.'

The men saw the king of the Djinn nod in agreement at these words and they felt afraid that perhaps the king would be persuaded by the mule's arguments and order men to free all the animals in their possession. What arguments could they put forward to show that such a decision would be unjust?

'We could say,' said one of them, 'that the animals belong to us, that they are our property like any other of our possessions which we have inherited from our fathers and forefathers. The animals are no different in this way from our houses, and nobody would ask us to give them up.'

'But what if we are asked to produce deeds, as with a house, or contracts, or to bring witnesses to prove that the animals are our property?' said another man.

'We must prepare our answers and be ready to argue our case against these animals,' the men agreed among themselves.

The animals, on the other hand, knew that the humans were more eloquent and had more experience in talking in public than the animals. They therefore decided that the best thing to do was for each group of animals to choose one of their number to be a spokesman at the court of the king of the Djinn.

So the animals divided themselves into seven different groups.

First, there were the farm animals, like cows and sheep and horses, who had already chosen the mule as their spokesman.

The second group was made up of the beasts of prey, those animals who hunt other animals and feed off their flesh.

The third group consisted of the birds of prey, those birds that eat the flesh of other birds or of animals.

Then, for the fourth group, there were the ordinary birds.

The fifth group were all the insects, such as bees, that are to be found in swarms.

The sixth group consisted of all those animals that crawl.

The seventh and last group were all those animals who live in the waters of the seas or of lakes and rivers.

In order that he might be able to come to a decision in the quarrel that had broken out between the animals and man, the king of the Djinn, having heard that the animals had formed themselves into seven different groups, gave instructions that a messenger should be sent to each of their kings asking them to choose someone to be their spokesman and representative at his court.

4

THE LION

When the messenger came to the lion, king of the beasts of prey, he explained to him how it was that some of the animals had complained to the king of the Djinn about man's bad treatment of them and that man was claiming that he was the master of all the animals and that they were his slaves.

'But that is ridiculous!' roared the lion. 'Why, with one charge from me I could send them flying in all directions. With one bite of my jaws I could separate a man's head from his body. With a single blow from my paw I could hurl a man to the ground so hard that he would never get up again.'

'Men claim that strength and courage do not prove anything,' explained the messenger. 'Men say they have other qualities that make them superior to animals and that they have invented special weapons for defending themselves against the

strongest and fiercest of animals — and for attacking them too. Now it has been decided that man and the animals must argue their case before the king of the Djinn and his judges, who will then decide whether man is right in his claim that he is the master of all the animals and they his slaves. So, great king, will you be the spokesman of the beasts of prey at the court of the king of the Djinn?'

The lion told the messenger that he would want to choose the most suitable of his subjects to be their spokesman. He then called all the beasts of prey together so that he might choose the animal with the necessary intelligence and eloquence for presenting their case in the best possible way. Soon there were gathered together in front of the lion all the leopards and cheetahs and jackals and wolves and foxes, and all the many other beasts of prey — animals who use claws and teeth for hunting and killing the animals whose flesh they eat.

'Who thinks himself best suited to represent us at the court of the king of the Djinn?' asked the lion of them.

The first one to come forward was the wolf.

'If you want someone capable of sudden and fierce attacks, then I am the one for you,' said the wolf.

'No,' said the lion, king of the beasts of prey.

Then the cat stood up and said, 'If you want someone who is clever at purring and making himself loved and trusted, then I'm the one for you.'

'No,' said the lion, king of the beasts of prey.

Next the dog leapt to his feet and said: 'If you want someone who can wag his tail and bark and look friendly, then I'm the one for you.'

'No,' said the lion, king of the beasts of prey, for he found that none of

these animals was the right one to represent them at the court of the king of the Djinn. He therefore asked his minister, the leopard, for his opinion.

'Your majesty,' replied the leopard, 'there is no one more suited to this task than the wise and experienced jackal.'

So the lion turned to the jackal and said, 'Are you willing to go as our spokesman and representative to the court of the king of the Djinn?'

'Your majesty,' said the jackal, 'I hear and I obey. I am at your majesty's service.'

'You shall be well rewarded if you are successful,' roared the lion, king of the beasts of prey.

'There is one difficulty, your majesty,' said the jackal.

'And what is that?' asked the lion, king of the beasts of prey.

'It is that among us animals are enemies of our own kind who are traitors to other animals.'

'What do you mean by that and who are these enemies you talk of?' demanded the lion, king of the beasts of prey.

'Dogs, your majesty,' answered the jackal. 'Dogs, your majesty, have made their homes in the houses of men. They have even learnt how to eat the same strange foods that man eats. Dogs will eat fruit and vegetables, bread, cheese and butter, and all kinds of sweet things — foods that no self-respecting

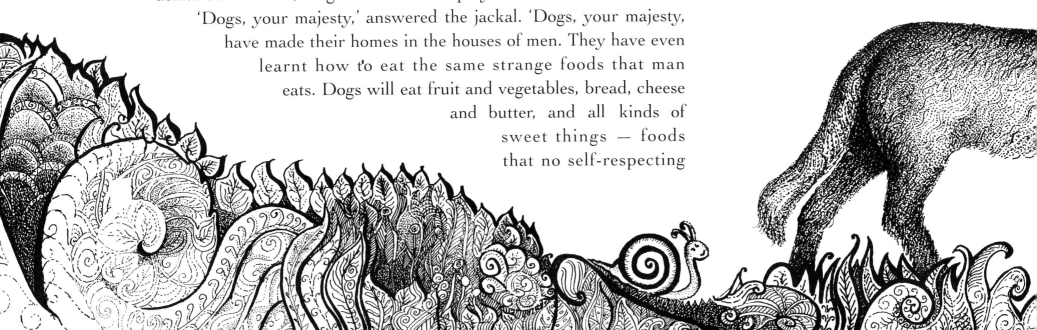

beast of prey would go anywhere near, not if he was dying of hunger. Dogs are very proud of their close relationship with man and so they treat as enemies any animal who seems to them to want to take away their special position in the hearts of men. And the reason why dogs get on so well with men and like living with them is that they share many of men's worst qualities: men and dogs are both greedy, both resentful of what others have, both miserly by nature.'

The lion nodded his great head.

'You are right about dogs,' he said. 'Though they belong to our group of animals, the beasts of prey, they are enemies to us and would certainly betray us to their human friends if ever they have the chance. And are there, O noble jackal, any other beasts of prey who are by nature eaters of meat, carnivores like us, and who, like the dogs, have become friends of men and live in their houses?'

'There are the cats,' answered the jackal. 'Cats, though loving meat, also greatly enjoy the many strange foods that humans eat.'

'And do the cats have a different life from the dogs?' asked the lion. 'You say that they too live in men's houses.'

'Your majesty,' answered the jackal, 'while both dogs and cats inhabit the houses of men and are his constant companions, it is clear that in many ways cats have a better life. While dogs are often forced to live outside men's houses and are sometimes tied up, cats spend most of their time inside the houses. Cats sleep in the same chairs and sofas as their masters use, and sometimes even on their beds. They are given many titbits from their masters' tables, and being small and nimble, are skilled at stealing food. All in all, they have an even better life than dogs and come and go as they please and are

never tied up. These are men's two great friends and allies, and it is no wonder that there is such hostility and rivalry between them, for they both spend all their time and energy trying to gain favours from their masters. I should mention that, while I have nothing to fear from cats, dogs in particular are great enemies of mine — I am sure I shall find that some men have brought dogs with them to the court of
the king of the Djinn.'

'May Allah protect you, O noble jackal, from the treachery of dogs!' roared the lion. 'And may Allah grant you a safe journey

to the
court of the king of the Djinn
when you go there as our spokesman.'

5

THE BIRDS CHOOSE THEIR

SPOKESMAN

The messenger of the king of the Djinn, after his visit to the lion, came to the simurg, that large fabulous winged creature who was king of the birds. The messenger told the king of the birds about the dispute between the animals and man and that all the various groups of animals were to choose one of their number to represent them at the court of the king of the Djinn. So a command was sent out that all the birds, from land and sea and mountain and plain, must present themselves before the great simurg, king of the birds. When they were all present, the king said to his minister, the peacock, 'Which, in your opinion, O minister, is the best bird to be our spokesman before the king of the Djinn?'

The peacock proudly spread his beautiful tail of wonderfully coloured feathers and answered, 'O majesty, there are many birds with excellent qualities who could act as our spokesman.'

28

'Tell me about some of them,' ordered the king of the birds.

'There is the hoopoe, your majesty,' answered the peacock. 'The hoopoe was a friend to the great King Solomon and it is said that he is the only bird with the power to see water through the earth. Also, he is continually bobbing his head up and down as though saying his prayers.'

'He is truly an admirable bird,' said the king of the birds. 'Are there any others?'

'Then there is the cock,' answered the peacock. 'He has the noble task of calling man at daybreak to perform his early morning prayers, waking up the whole district with his loud call at the first light of dawn.'

'He is truly an admirable bird,' agreed the king of the birds. 'Are there any others?'

'Well, your majesty,' answered the peacock, 'there is the homing pigeon. He is able to carry letters and messages over long distances. The Almighty has blessed him with the miraculous gift of knowing his way back to his home however far away from it he may be released.'

'He is truly an admirable bird,' agreed the king of the birds. 'Are there any others?'

The peacock again spread out his beautiful tail as he walked several paces to and fro in thought. 'In addition, your majesty,' he said, 'there is of course the swallow. He is very skilful at building his nest, which he constructs of mud against the walls of houses inhabited by humans. Thus he can be said to be a neighbour of man. Also, he is one of the fastest flying birds and travels to faraway countries, spending the summer in cool climates and the winter in warm ones.'

'He is truly an admirable bird,' said the king of the birds and once again he enquired of the peacock whether there was anyone else he could suggest to represent

them at the court of the king of the Djinn.

'I had forgotten to mention to your majesty the nightingale,' said the peacock. 'He has the most melodious voice of any bird. His body is not large but the song that he sings is the most beautiful of all and would surely win the heart of any listener.'

The simurg, king of the birds, thanked the peacock for his suggestions and was silent for a while as he thought about whom he would choose. Then he addressed the birds and said, 'We birds are famous for our different calls and songs and I think you would all agree that it is the nightingale who has the sweetest song of all. I shall therefore ask him who is our greatest singer to represent us at the court of the king of the Djinn.'

All the birds flapped their wings in agreement.

'Go!' said the king of the birds to the nightingale. 'Go and may Allah be with you on your journey and at the court. Rely on Allah, for He is the best Helper and Protector.'

6

THE BEE

When the messenger from the king of the Djinn left the birds, he made his way to the bee, the king of the swarming creatures. So the bee immediately commanded that all the different sorts of swarming insects should attend before him so that they could choose someone to represent them at the court of the king of the Djinn. Thus there gathered together the wasps and flies and mosquitoes and butterflies and moths, all those small-bodied creatures with wings who have neither feathers, wool nor hair and who mostly live onlya short time, dying in the extreme heat of summer or the bitter cold of winter. When they were all before him the bee explained to them about the quarrel between the animals and man because of man's claim that he was their master and that all animals were his slaves.

'And why does man think himself so superior to us that he can regard us as his slaves?' asked the wasp in surprise.

'It is because of their large bodies and great strength,' answered the messenger from the king of the Djinn.

'But size and strength are not everything,' said the wasp. 'Sometimes you can see a great powerful man all dressed up in his shining armour, with his sword, his lance and his bow and arrows, all ready to do battle against an army of enemies. Then, all of a sudden, one of us happens to get under his armour and stabs him with a sting that is no bigger than the point of a needle. The next moment this great soldier lets out a squeal of pain and has forgotten all about the battle and his enemies. He has thoughts only for the pain he is feeling from the sting of one of us wasps, who are no bigger than the tip of his little finger. Soon he has such a swelling on his body that he can hardly hold his sword with which he was intending to kill his enemies.'

'That is so,' said the wise bee, king of the swarming creatures.

'And is it not true,' said the leader of the mosquitoes,

'that a human can be sitting in his chair or
lying on his bed and all we need to do is
fly all around him, attacking as we
choose any uncovered parts of his
body till we make it impossible for
him to rest or go to sleep? He will
of course try to kill us by striking at
us with his enormous hands but
generally all he succeeds in doing is
slapping his own face.'

'That is so,' said the wise bee,
king of the swarming creatures. 'These
are all signs that man, despite his great size
and strength, is not so powerful as he thinks and that even the smallest of the
animals is able to get the better of him. So let us choose one of our number to
represent us and put forward such arguments to the king of the Djinn.'

But when all the different kinds of insects began discussing among
themselves who would be their best spokesman, they came to the decision
that there was no one more clever and eloquent than their king himself,
the wise bee.

'Would your majesty be so good as to represent us?' they
asked the bee. 'We do not like to ask you such a
thing because we know how long and dangerous
a journey it is to the court of the
king of the Djinn, and for
this reason we

would prefer you to choose one of us, your loyal subjects.'

The bee, having listened joyfully to what his subjects had to say, immediately answered them. 'If you are of the opinion that I am the one to be your spokesman, then I am only too happy to make the journey. I am a strong flyer and will thus be able to bear the hardships of a long flight better than many of you.'

So after all the insects had wished him a safe journey and a speedy return, the wise bee flew off to the court of the king of the Djinn.

7

THE BIRDS OF PREY

It was to the griffin, that fabulous bird who was the king of the birds of prey, that the messenger of the king of the Djinn next went. He told him that the birds of prey, who hunt and kill so that they can have the meat which is their food, should also choose a spokesman. So every bird of prey with talons and a hooked beak — eagles, hawks, falcons, vultures, owls and others — gathered before the griffin.

The king of the birds of prey was told by his minister that the owl was certainly the best bird to represent them.

'Why is that?' asked the king of the birds of prey.

'Because,' said his minister, 'all the other birds of prey are afraid of man and keep as far away from him as they can. They would therefore be nervous at court and would not be any good at speaking in the presence of so many men. The owl, on the other hand, is a neighbour to man, for he often chooses to take as his home some old building that man has abandoned. Also the owl is well known for his piety and humility, doing his hunting by night and fasting throughout the day.'

So the king of the birds of prey addressed the owl, saying, 'Are you willing to go to the court of the king of the Djinn to represent us there?'

The owl blinked his eyes as he thought for a while and then answered, 'I consider it a great honour to be asked to represent us birds of prey. It is of course true that we owls often make our homes close to where men are living, but I do not think I am the right person to argue our case against human beings.'

'And why not?' asked the king of the birds of prey, surprised that the owl was not willing to act as their spokesman.

'It is no secret,' said the owl, 'that human beings do not like us and that the hooting noise we make at night brings fear to their hearts. As men have no liking for us, I feel that some other bird should be our spokesman.'

'And whom would you propose?' asked the king of the birds of prey.

'I can think of no one better than the falcon,' answered the owl immediately. 'Though not as large and powerful as the eagle, who is much respected by men, the falcons and hawks are greatly loved by them. Man trains and uses them for hunting, a sport which he much enjoys, and spends many hours talking to his falcons as they sit on his wrist, where he feeds them with pieces of raw meat and strokes them lovingly. Great sums of money are paid by kings and princes for

falcons that are strong fliers and can swoop down like lightning from the skies upon other birds or rabbits. And when the falcon has killed his prey, his master takes it for himself and rewards the falcon with words of praise and affection.'

So the king of the birds of prey agreed that the best possible spokesman for them was the falcon, that bird so highly prized by man. And all the birds of prey said a prayer for the falcon, asking Allah the Almighty that he might be given the gift of eloquence at the court of the king of the Djinn.

8

THE WATER ANIMALS

The next group of animals visited by the messenger of the king of the Djinn was that of the water animals. To their king, the powerful sea-serpent, he told of the dispute between the animals and man and asked him to choose a spokesman. So the sea-serpent summoned all the many kinds of creatures that live wholly or mainly in water, such as turtles, crocodiles, dolphins, whales, crabs and frogs.

It was at once suggested that the whale was the most suitable person to represent the water animals because he was the largest, the most handsome and also the strongest swimmer. Another reason for choosing the whale was that he was well thought of by man because of the way in which the whale had given refuge in his great belly to the Prophet Jonah, upon whom be peace, and had delivered him to the safety of dry land.

But when the whale was asked about this he said, 'What you say about me is true, but how could I go to the court of the king of the Djinn when

Allah the Almighty has not created me with feet for travelling on land, or with wings for flying through the air? As you all know, I can live only in the great oceans and if I am cast up on dry land I soon die. I think that the turtle, who can both swim in the sea and walk upon the land, is better suited to the task. He can breathe both in the air and under water, also he is a most sensitive and patient animal.'

So the sea-serpent turned to the turtle and asked him what he thought about the whale's suggestion.

'I am most honoured that the whale should suggest me as spokesman for the water animals, but I must be honest and say that I do not think I am the right person. First of all, I am a very slow walker and it is a long journey to the court of the king of the Djinn. Also, and this is most important, I am a very poor public speaker and would not be able to present our case well.'

Then someone suggested that the crab was the most suitable spokesman. Having many legs, he was an excellent walker and he had strong claws to use against his enemies and was covered all over with protective armour like a warrior.

The sea-serpent turned to the crab and asked him if he was willing to be their spokesman.

'Your majesty must excuse me,' said the crab firmly, 'but I do not consider that I am the right person for the task. In His infinite wisdom the Almighty has made me ugly-looking in the sight of men and other animals, though He has compensated me in other ways. Human beings, however, are much concerned with outward appearances and I do not think they would take seriously an animal who walks sideways and who has his eyes built into his shoulders.'

The sea-serpent quickly assured the crab that he for one found the crab a most attractive creature and could see nothing wrong in his walking sideways or having his eyes on his shoulders. 'Feeling as you do, however,' he went on, 'who would you suggest we send to the court of the king of the Djinn as our spokesman?'

'Your majesty, why not the crocodile?' answered the crab. 'He is a fine walker and can even run very swiftly. His mouth is large, and he has many sharp teeth, a powerful body and an appearance that strikes fear into his enemies.'

But when the sea-serpent asked the crocodile about being their spokesman, the crocodile replied, 'Much as I would like to be of service to your majesty and to my fellow creatures who live in water, I do not feel that I

possess the necessary qualifications to be a spokesman. I am, for a start, a very irritable and short-tempered person and would soon lose my patience when faced with so many men and animals.'

The sea-serpent then asked the crocodile if there was anyone particular he could suggest to represent them.

'Indeed, your majesty!' the crocodile at once replied. 'I would without hesitation put forward the frog as the best person for such a delicate job. He is dignified and patient — unlike myself. He is also, as you all know, a most pious person who, in the darkness of night, croaks forth his praise of the Almighty. In addition, he often lives close to men and they have no fear of him.'

When he was asked by the sea-serpent whether he was willing to travel to the court of the king of the Djinn as their spokesman, the frog answered, 'If your majesty agrees that I am the right person to represent the water animals, then I shall of course obey you. All I would ask is that you all give praise to the Almighty and pray to Him to grant me His guidance in the task that lies before me.'

Then all the water animals said a prayer for the frog, asking that he might have a safe journey and a speedy return and that Allah the Almighty might put wise thoughts in his head and eloquent words in his mouth when his time came to speak.

9

THE CRAWLING CREATURES

The last visit that the messenger of the king of the Djinn paid was to the dragon, king of the crawling animals. Once again he explained about the quarrel between the animals and man and about the necessity for the crawling animals to choose a representative to send to the court of the king of the Djinn.

So the dragon summoned all the crawling animals to appear before him: the snakes and scorpions and lizards and cockroaches and spiders and crickets and ants and all the different kinds of worms and every other creature that crawls upon the earth.

When they were all gathered together their king, the dragon, looked at them and was astonished at the great number of different shapes and sizes in which the Creator had formed them. He also felt deep pity for these creatures drawn up before him, many of whom were deaf and

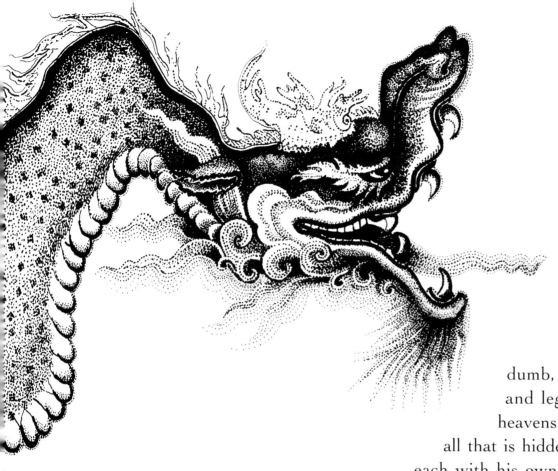

dumb, blind and mute, while some were without hands
and legs, wings, beaks and claws. He cried out to the
heavens: 'O most Merciful One, who sees, hears and knows
all that is hidden, You who created them and provides for them,
each with his own food, who gives them life and then brings them
death, be our Guardian and our Helper, guide us and lead us, O
Possessor of the Great Throne.'

And all the crawling creatures cried out together, 'Amen, Amen,
O Lord of the Worlds.'

The cricket, seeing how distressed the dragon was by the
apparent helplessness of the creatures over whom he ruled, got up on
to a nearby wall and began to play his stringed instrument and blow
on his musical pipe, making lovely tunes with which to praise Allah

and His Oneness. Then the cricket spoke to the king of the crawling creatures and said, 'Do not be so sad, your majesty, about the small and puny bodies that many of your subjects have. You should know that the Almighty, the Creator of them and the Provider for them, has more love for them than a mother and a father have for their own children. When the Almighty made the numberless animals in all their various shapes and sizes, some large and strong, others small and weak, in His wisdom He gave equally to each one, so that every one of His creatures is able to find his own food and to protect himself against his enemies.'

'And how is it,' asked the dragon, the king of the crawling creatures, 'that both the weak and the strong are able to protect themselves against their enemies?'

So the cricket explained this with the following words: 'Those

that are big and strong, like the elephants and the lions, defend themselves with their claws and teeth and tusks. Others, like gazelles and rabbits, who are fleet of foot, defend themselves by running away from their enemies. Yet others, like the birds, take to the air, while those who live in water swim away to safety. Then there are those, like ants and mice, who hide themselves in holes in the ground. About this the Almighty has said in the Holy Qur'an. "An ant said: 'O ants, enter your houses lest Solomon and his soldiers destroy you, without their being aware.'" Others of His creatures, like crabs and turtles and snails, have been given special armour that protects them from their enemies, while the hedgehog, for instance, rolls himself into a spiky ball and thus comes to no harm. Praise to the Creator for His blessings!'

'May Allah bless you!' exclaimed the king of the crawling creatures, addressing the cricket in gratitude for having removed from him his feelings of sadness. 'May Allah be praised for having fashioned someone so intelligent and so clever with words. It is you, O cricket, who must be our spokesman at the court of the king of the Djinn.'

'I hear and I obey, your majesty,' answered the cricket.

So all the crawling creatures wished the cricket a safe journey and a speedy return.

10

AT THE COURT OF THE KING OF THE DJINN

The next day all the representatives of the animals, together with the representatives of the men, gathered before the king of the Djinn at his court. The judges of the Djinn and their learned men were also present. Men and animals came from all parts of the island to hear what the various spokesmen would say and hear the king of the Djinn give judgement in the case.

The king of the Djinn looked to right and left and saw these many creatures of different appearances and for some time he was speechless with wonder. Then he turned to one of the learned men and said, 'Do you not see all these wonderful creatures that the All-Merciful has made and with which He has peopled the world?'

'Yes, your majesty,' said the learned man. 'I see them with the eyes of my head, and I see their Maker with the eyes of my heart. Your majesty is astonished at them, but I am astonished at the great power of the Creator who has fashioned them and who provides for them, each with his own needs. It is Allah who has made all His creatures: Djinn, humans, angels, and every kind of animal. Praise be to Allah who has put faith into our hearts and has guided us to Islam and has made men His viceregents and representatives on this earth. And praise be to Allah who has given us a king of such learning, wisdom and goodness. Now listen to the king of the Djinn and answer truthfully any questions he may have.'

Then the king of the Djinn gazed at all the men and animals drawn up before him. To one side he noticed the jackal, who was standing next to the donkey and looking unhappy and frightened because there were so many dogs, his great enemies, standing nearby with their human owners.

'Who are you?' asked the king of the Djinn.

'I am the jackal, your majesty. I am here as the spokesman of the beasts of prey,' said the jackal.

'Who sent you here?' asked the king of the Djinn.

'Our king, your majesty,' said the jackal.

'And who is he?' asked the king of the Djinn.

'The great and powerful lion,' said the jackal.

'And in what lands does he live?' asked the king of the Djinn.

'In jungles and deserts, your majesty,' said the jackal.

'And who are his subjects?' asked the king of the Djinn.

'Your majesty, we the jackals and the wolves, the leopards and the foxes are his subjects, all those who fight with tooth and claw and eat meat.'

The king of the Djinn then asked the jackal whether the lion, their king, behaved well and fairly towards his subjects.

'Very well and fairly, your majesty,' answered the jackal.

The king of the Djinn asked the same question of all the other spokesmen of the various groups of animals and enquired who their kings were and the places in which they lived.

Then the king of the Djinn noticed the frog, who was riding on a piece of wood near the sea shore. The frog, in his croaking voice, like the rest of the animals in their different ways and voices, was giving prayers of praise to the Almighty.

'And who are you?' asked the king of the Djinn.

'The frog, spokesman of the water animals, your majesty,' answered the frog.

'And who are the water animals?' asked the king of the Djinn.

'The crocodiles and dolphins and whales and crabs and the other many sea creatures whose number is known to Allah alone,' said the frog.

Then the frog asked permission to speak on behalf of the creatures of water and all other animals, and he began by saying that it was ridiculous for man to claim that humans were the masters and that all animals were his slaves.

'Your majesty,' continued the frog, 'no animal is superior to another. It is only that we are all different from one another, for Allah in His wisdom has made us so. As you know, your majesty, it can happen that even the biggest and most powerful animal can be bitten by some tiny insect and die. The same is true of man. There is no difference between man and us animals in this. Sometimes man is the eater, but at other times it is he who is eaten. Man's end, whatever form it may take, is the same as that of any animal. All of us are born only to die. What has deceived the humans into thinking themselves superior is that they have succeeded in making prisoners of farm animals, who are harmless and do not bite or sting, and now they are showing them no mercy day or night. Also they cruelly hunt many wild animals and birds for food.'

The king of the Djinn listened with great attention to the words of the frog and saw that there was much truth in what he said.

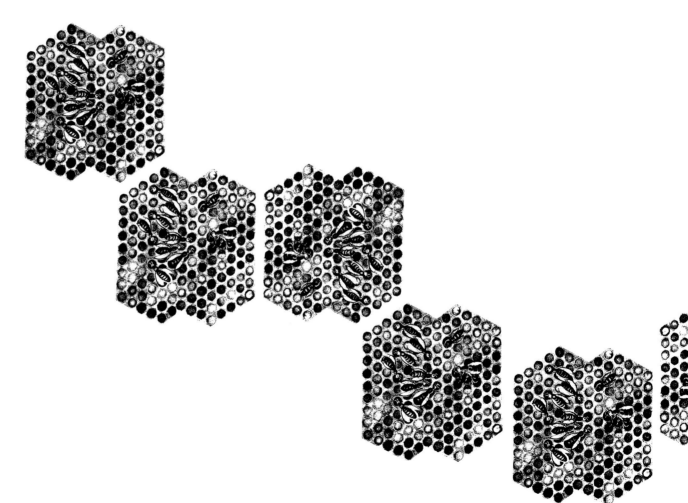

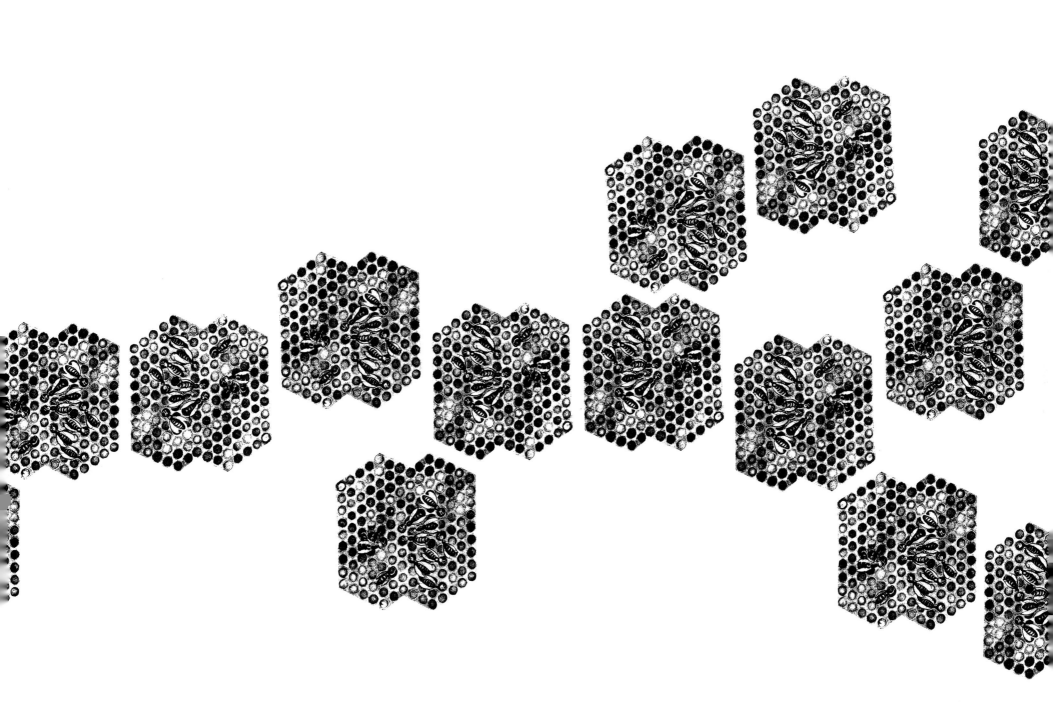

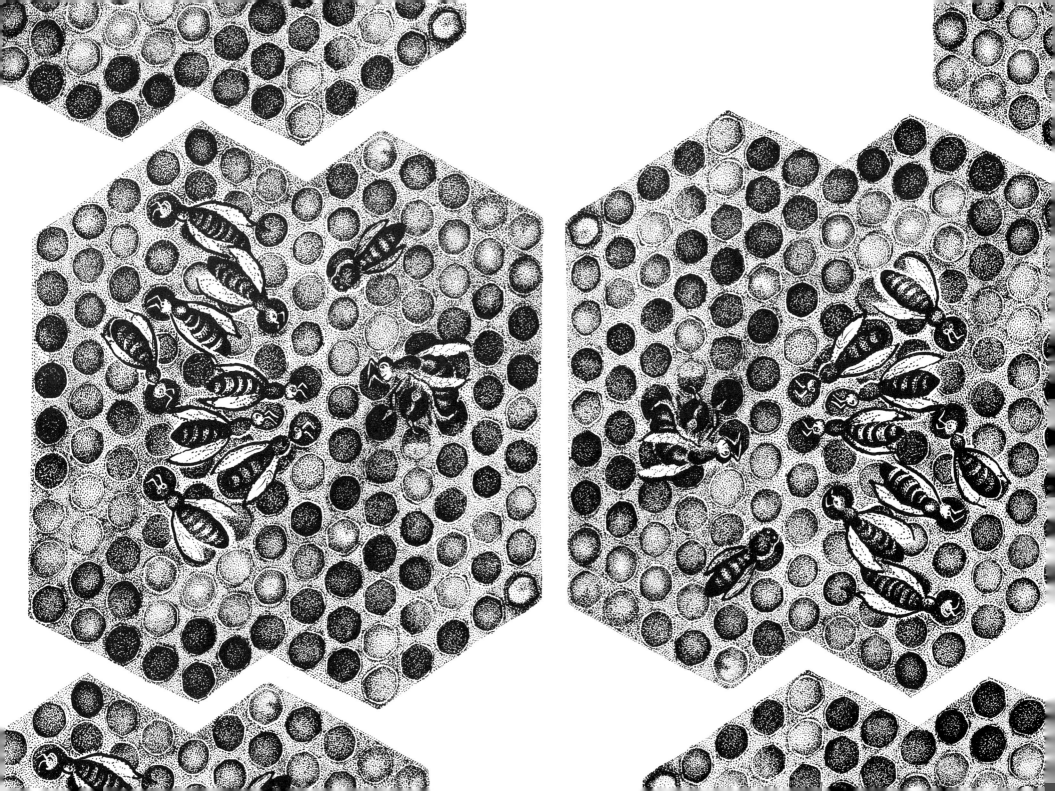

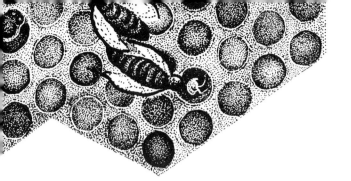

11

THE BEE TELLS HIS STORY

When the king of the Djinn had fully considered what the frog had said, he looked at the ranks of men drawn up in front of him and asked, 'Who is your king?'

'We have many kings, your majesty,' answered one of the humans.

'How is that?' asked the king of the Djinn. 'These animals have a king for each group of animals, while you tell me that humans have many kings.'

'That is so, your majesty,' said the man, 'for human lives are more complicated than those of animals. Human kings need armies to defend their lands against their enemies. They also need generals and ministers and governors and tax collectors, and judges and scholars learned in the teachings of religion, for there is no kingdom which does not have its own religious rules by which its subjects can live in happiness. In the same way, different countries need separate kings to govern them, and there are many states and countries on this earth, and each one differs from the others in language, beliefs and customs. It is thus necessary to have a great number of human kings for all these countries and peoples.'

'Now I understand,' said the king of the Djinn, 'why humans have so many kings while each group of animals finds it sufficient to have a single king. But do these human kings differ in any way from the kings that the animals have?'

'They do, your majesty,' answered the man.

'Explain to me in what ways,' said the king of the Djinn.

'All human kings,' answered the man, 'are God's representatives on earth. It is Allah who allows them to rule over His lands and who makes them responsible for His creatures. Allah is the Ruler of the universe and it is He who rules over all creatures, from the very highest to the very lowest.'

The king of the Djinn, having listened with interest to what he had been told about human kings, now turned his gaze on the many animals ranged in front of him. Suddenly he heard a buzzing sound and there, hovering in mid-air and moving his tiny wings with a sound that was like the highest note of a violin, was the bee. It was in this way that the bee sang the praises of his Lord.

'And who are you?' asked the king of the Djinn.

'I am the bee, your majesty, the spokesman of the swarming creatures,' answered the bee. 'I am also their king.'

'Why, then,' said the king of the Djinn, 'if you are the king of the swarming creatures, did you not send one of your subjects as the other animal groups have done and spared yourself the trouble of coming to my court?'

'My subjects,' answered the bee, 'decided that I should represent them at your majesty's court, and as their king I felt it was only right that I who have been granted the ability to fly long distances should myself undertake the journey.'

The king of the Djinn was amazed that the bee should have shown such consideration for his subjects and have undergone the fatigue and dangers of coming to his court.

'Tell me about yourself,' said the king of the Djinn, 'that I may know something about the only king from among the animals who has put the comfort and safety of his subjects before his own comfort and safety.'

To this the wise bee answered, 'Allah the Almighty has granted to me many gifts. He has given me a body which, though small, performs all the functions required of it; upon my shoulders He has placed silky wings with which I can fly through the air at speed. He has also given me a sting which is as sharp as a thorn and which I can use as a weapon to drive off those who seek to do me harm. Most important of all, my Creator has made it possible for me to keep within my body the liquid I take from the blossoms of flowers and to change it into sweet and beneficial honey, from which I and my children can feed and which I can store so that we can use it as food during the hard days of winter when there are no flowers.'

The king of the Djinn was delighted at the way the bee told of the blessings his Lord had bestowed on him.

'And in what kinds of places do the bees make their homes?' the king of the Djinn asked him.

'Both in high mountains and in valleys full of trees, anywhere in fact where there are flowers from which to make our honey,' answered the bee. 'Some of us also make our homes close to where humans live.'

'And do you find that humans make good neighbours?' asked the king of the Djinn.

57

'Not at all,' said the wise bee, shaking his tiny head. 'Sometimes the humans come to search for us. If we are not able to defend ourselves against them, they destroy our homes, kill our children and steal the honey which we have made and stored up. They take all the honey and leave none for us. They excuse themselves for doing these cruel things by claiming that they are our masters and we their slaves and that everything we do must be for their benefit and not for ourselves.'

The king of the Djinn listened with great attention to what the bee, so small in size and so large in wisdom, had to say. The other animals also heard the sad story the bee told about the way in which humans treated these industrious and peaceful creatures.

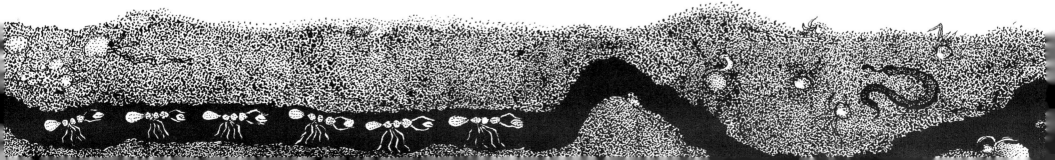

12

THE BEE'S ELOQUENCE

The king of the Djinn, having listened to several spokesmen from among the animals, now spoke to the men who were gathered in his court.

'You have heard,' he said to them, 'how the animals have spoken against you. You have heard their complaints about the cruel treatment they receive from you. Have you anything to say to show that you are in fact masters of all these animals and that you therefore have the right to treat them as you wish?'

One of the men now rose to his feet and told the king of the Djinn about the many sciences and kinds of knowledge that men possessed, and

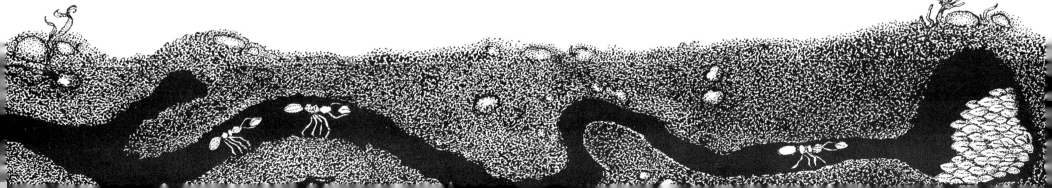

how men worked ceaselessly with their minds and bodies to increase
their knowledge and to improve their lives through industry,
agriculture and trade. All these
things   were   proof,
he   said,   that

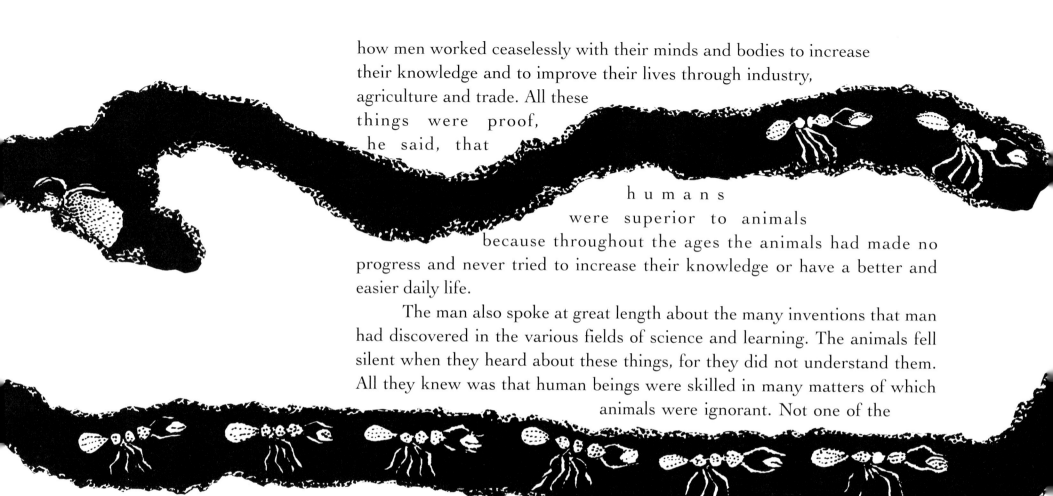

h u m a n s
were   superior   to   animals
because throughout the ages the animals had made no
progress and never tried to increase their knowledge or have a better and
easier daily life.

The man also spoke at great length about the many inventions that man
had discovered in the various fields of science and learning. The animals fell
silent when they heard about these things, for they did not understand them.
All they knew was that human beings were skilled in many matters of which
animals were ignorant. Not one of the

animals could find anything to say
against man's reasons for claiming that humans were superior to animals.
Once again it was the wise little bee who spoke out on behalf of all animals.
'Your majesty,' said the bee, 'these humans say that they possess
knowledge of various sciences about which we animals know nothing. This
is in a way true, but men are of course talking only from their own point of

view — and it is well known about man that he never sees anybody else's point of view. If he were capable of looking at things from other points of view, he would realize at once that we animals manage our lives perfectly well without all the sciences of which man boasts, for we animals have our own kinds of knowledge which are suited to our particular ways of life. Man should be able to see that we animals are well able to organize our lives properly, quite as well in fact as humans do.'

'Give us some examples, O wise bee,' said the king of the Djinn.

'One example I can give,' said the bee, 'is the way in which we bees organize ourselves, how we make our small, precisely built houses, each one placed directly against the next, and we make them without the use of any instruments or knowledge of geometry. Look at the manner in which we appoint certain bees to act as porters and others to be guards. Look at the way we gather wax from the leaves of trees with our legs and honey with our lips from the blossoms of plants. Look at how we and our children feed during the

winter from the honey we have stored, and how, once spring has come and the weather grows warmer and the flowers open their petals, out we go again to the fields. So it is that we live in peace and harmony with nature and in accordance with the teachings given to us by our Maker.'

When the king of the Djinn asked him if he had other examples of the way in which God's creatures organize themselves, though they possess no books or knowledge of any of the sciences, the bee answered: 'Your majesty, the wonders of the Almighty can never be told. Nature is full of instances where the Creator of all things has arranged that His creatures can organize their lives in accordance with their needs. Take for example the ants and the way in which they build whole towns inside the ground, with tunnels, passageways and storerooms which they fill with grain. See how methodically they build these houses and set about collecting the food they want for storing. If one of them goes out in search of food and finds something which is too heavy for him to carry alone, he returns to his fellow ants with the news so that several of them may go back with him and all together they drag it to where it can be stored. If humans would only study the lives of these tiny beings, they would discover that ants too have their own sorts of knowledge which are of direct use to them in their daily lives. Humans would also do well to study the silk worms who live in high mountainous places and make their homes in mulberry trees, whose leaves are their food, and how they are able to encircle their frail little bodies with that delicate thread which man takes for himself and uses as silk.'

The wise bee explained that these and other crawling and creeping creatures lay eggs and bring up their young with the same care and love as humans do. Unlike humans, though, they expect no thanks from their children. It is in their nature to multiply and to make certain that their children shall continue on after they are dead. Thus they seek no gratitude from their young simply for doing what nature has taught them. How, then, can humans claim that they are superior to such creatures?

13

THE NIGHTINGALE SPEAKS

The king of the Djinn congratulated the bee on his great eloquence, then turned to the humans and asked them if they had anything more to say that would show they were superior to the animals.

A man rose to his feet and spoke about the qualities that were peculiar to the human race and which proved that they were the masters of animals. He spoke of the many varieties of delicious food that men prepare for themselves, of the fine clothes made of cotton, wool and silk that they wear, and of the costly furniture and carpets with which they fill their houses.

The nightingale, the spokesman of the birds, had been sitting on the branch of a tree and singing in his beautiful voice as he listened to what the man was saying. Now he decided to reply to this man.

'All this luxurious living,' said the nightingale, 'all these expensive clothes, all these fine foods and drinks and great houses in which man lives are in fact nothing but causes of worry and distress to him.'

'And how is that?' enquired the king of the Djinn. 'Explain what you say.'

The nightingale then continued as follows: 'The complicated lives that humans have chosen for themselves, your majesty, require ceaseless toil. Always they are having to do such work as ploughing the ground and sowing seed, irrigating their fields, digging wells, harvesting and transporting their crop, then preparing and cooking the foods they have grown. Always they are working so as to make the money with which to provide themselves and their families with all the luxuries they consider essential to their lives, and of which the animals are in no need. Never are men satisfied, so they are always striving to have more of everything. For this reason they suffer the tortures of greed, envy and miserliness.'

The king of the Djinn nodded his head in agreement with what the nightingale had said, then the nightingale went on to explain how different were the lives of birds, how simple and uncomplicated.

'Our food, your majesty,' said the nightingale, 'springs up through the earth where the seeds lie till they are nourished by the rains that come down from the heavens. Our food consists of berries and grasses and fruits. These are provided for us season by season, year after year, without any work from our bodies or our minds. We are satisfied with what the Almighty gives us and we do not strive to have more than this. When we have eaten our fill for the day we leave what is left over for the next day, or for other birds. We do not worry about the future or about having our homes broken into by thieves or robbers, so our nests have neither doors nor locks. This shows that we are noble and free, leading our lives in the way the Almighty has ordained.'

But directly the nightingale, spokesman of the birds, had finished speaking, a man rose to his feet. He pointed out that men had been favoured by the Almighty, for it was to them that Allah had sent His prophets and His revealed books, His commandments and prohibitions. Man makes himself pure and noble through performing his ablutions and his prayers, through fasting and giving in charity and through joining with his fellow men for the purpose of worship in mosques, churches and synagogues. All this, the man claimed, gave humans a special position among other creatures and showed their superiority.

The nightingale, having listened to the man's words, replied immediately, addressing himself to the humans who were sitting in the court of the king of the Djinn. 'If only you humans,' he said to them, 'gave more attention to what you say, if you only thought more carefully before speaking, you would know that your words are against you rather than for you. It is quite clear that all these commandments to pray and to fast, to give money in charity and to be kind to your fellow men, have been directed to mankind rather than to animals because you men so often behave wickedly. But we birds and animals have no desire to do evil actions and are therefore in no need of being encouraged to do good or of being warned against doing evil. As to performing ablutions before praying, this is required of men because of the evil desires and lusts in which they indulge by day and by night throughout the year. We animals, on the other hand, have our fixed times for copulation and are driven to it not by lust and pleasure but by the instinct to procreate and preserve our species. As you know, O humans, the prophets, may peace be upon them, are doctors for the illnesses of the soul, and it is obvious that it is only the sick who are in need of doctors. O humans, do you not see that it is you who are sick in your souls and need doctors?'

The nightingale stopped talking and looked round amongst the men, expecting that one of them would rise to his feet and argue against what he had said. When he saw that all of them were keeping silent, the nightingale continued, 'You say, O men, that charity has been made part of your religion. Is this not because you are all greedy by nature, seeking to collect around yourselves more and more of the things you like and hating to give them away to friends and neighbours, let alone to strangers? We birds, though, do not have such evil ways and live happily from day to day. As to the special buildings in which you go to worship, and special directions towards which you are commanded to pray, we have no need of such things. Wherever we turn there is the face of Allah, and all our movements are acts of worship and we are continually giving praise to the Almighty whenever we raise our voices in song.'

Night was beginning to fall, so the king of the Djinn wished everybody a good night's rest and commanded that they should all, men and animals, meet on the following morning, if such was the will of Allah.

14

THE MAN FROM MECCA AND MEDINA

The next day when everyone was gathered before him in his court, the king of the Djinn, having considered during the night the arguments that had been put to him by the spokesmen of the animals, now directed his words to the men.

'O humans, it has been shown to me that many of the things about which you boast are certainly not evidence that you are better than the animals and that they are your slaves. Rather should you understand that we are all slaves of the Almighty. It is He who has created all of us and it is He who has given some of us power over others. We have listened to what you have said about the many ways in which you see yourselves as superior to the animals and we have heard their replies. It is now your last chance, O humans, to put forward any other arguments you may have before we give our decision.'

There now rose to his feet a man from the Hijaz, a man who came from the land of the Holy Cities of Mecca and Medina.

'Your majesty,' he said, 'there is yet another way in which we humans differ from animals. It has not yet been mentioned by anyone, but I think that your majesty will see its great importance.

'Speak,' commanded the king of the Djinn, 'and let everyone listen to what the man from the land of the Holy Cities has to say.'

'Our Creator,' said the man from the Hijaz, 'the Lord of all living creatures, has promised that we humans, to the exclusion of everyone else, shall be raised up from our graves after the Day of Judgement. Allah the Almighty has promised us that we shall live for ever in His garden of Paradise, where we shall be close to His glorious presence. All of this is told in His Book, the Holy Qur'an. It is promised by Allah to mankind, but the animals are not included in this promise. Is this not proof, your majesty, that Allah has singled us out as masters and has given us the animals as our slaves?'

Once again it was the nightingale, spokesman of the birds, who answered. 'You are right, O man, in what you say,' said the nightingale, 'but it seems that you have forgotten — or choose not to mention — the other side of the Almighty's promise to mankind. You have not said that man, while being promised that he shall have the chance of being taken to Paradise and of living there happily for ever, may none the less find himself being cast into the burning fires of Hell and of being punished there for the sins he has committed during his lifetime. This too is clearly recounted in the Almighty's Book, the Holy Qur'an, side by side with the verses that tell of the joys of Paradise. Just as the possibility of going to Paradise has been given only to

you men, so too has the possibility of being confined in Hell. But we animals live neither in hope of the one, nor in fear of the other, for we have been promised no rewards and have been warned of no punishments. We do not therefore see that your position is in any way better than ours or that you have the right to consider yourselves our superiors.'

The nightingale, pleased with the manner in which he had spoken, stood up on the branch of the tree and raised his sweet voice in song. His singing was interrupted by the man from the land of the Holy Cities who had again jumped to his feet to address the king of the Djinn.

'Your majesty,' he said, 'this bird's arguments do not show the whole truth. He says that our position is no different from the position of animals because man may well go to Hell rather than to Heaven. In either case, though, we men shall enjoy eternal life. The nightingale should also have mentioned that if, at the Day of Judgement, the Almighty should decide that we have lived in accordance with His commands and the teachings of His Prophet, then we shall be rewarded with life everlasting in His Paradise, where we shall dwell with the prophets and saints, and with the blessed and the virtuous. If, though, judgement is given against us and we are placed by our Maker in the flames of Hell, we can still hope that the prophets, peace be upon them, and especially our beloved Muhammad, may the blessings and peace of Allah be upon him, will successfully plead for us with the Almighty so that we may be taken from the flames of Hell and be allowed to enjoy the pleasures of Paradise. This is something the nightingale failed to mention. In this most important of ways, your majesty, has man been favoured by the Almighty, and it is for this reason that we regard ourselves as masters and the animals as our slaves, to deal with as we think best.'

It was with this powerful argument that the man from the land of Mecca and Medina spoke on behalf of mankind, and the animals exchanged glances among themselves and found that they had nothing further to say. The king of the Djinn then thanked all the men and animals and informed them that he required time in which to consult with his judges and learned men before coming to a decision about something so important. He told the assembly that a great feast had been prepared for them, with all the special foods for the different animals and birds and insects, and with many delicacies for the men, and that after they had eaten their fill they should return to hear his verdict.

15

THE KING OF THE DJINN GIVES HIS VERDICT

When all the animals and men returned to the court of the king of the Djinn, they grouped themselves in anxious expectancy of the arrival of the king himself. Then the king of the Djinn entered, followed by his judges and learned men. He seated himself on the throne and, in the tense silence, exchanged a few words with the Djinn on either side of him before delivering his verdict.

'O assembly of men and animals, I and my advisers, having listened to your many eloquent speeches, have been much impressed by what the various spokesmen for mankind have said about their skills in the sciences and their deep learning, also about the progress they are continually making in all the fields of knowledge, matters which they claim give them the right to treat the animals as their inferiors and their slaves. It certainly does seem to us that man is in many respects superior to the animals.'

As the king of the Djinn said these words, the men who were seated in front of him turned to each other and began talking excitedly among themselves, for it seemed clear that the decision

was going to be given in their favour. One man even clapped his hands in delight, but the king of the Djinn frowned and called for silence.

'I have not finished what I have to say,' he told them, looking down sternly at the man who had interrupted him by clapping. 'Now, while it is true that men have achieved many things that are outside the power of animals, the spokesmen for the animals have put their case in a very convincing manner. They have shown that they are in no need of many of the skills and knowledge possessed by man and that in regard to their own special needs they are perfectly able to lead full and enjoyable lives. The animals have also argued that they are free of many of the bad qualities to be found in men such as greed, envy and miserliness. There is no doubt whatsoever that the animals in these matters are far superior to men and it would therefore be only right that the men should be slaves to the animals and not the other way round as men claim.'

It was now the turn of the animals to feel happy, while the men were sad and looked down at their feet, for they knew that what had been said about their bad qualities was only too true. Everyone became quiet again as the king of the Djinn called for silence.

'We found,' continued the king of the Djinn, 'that it has been very difficult to come to a decision in this case, for both sides have put up strong arguments to show their superiority. It seemed to us that neither side, neither the men nor the animals, was superior, merely that each was different from the other. But then the man from the land of the Holy Cities of Mecca and Medina presented the final argument on man's behalf. It was only then that we became convinced of the superiority of man, for man, as we have been told in the scriptures, is unique and different from all other animals in one very important respect.'

The men and animals waited in deep silence for the king of the Djinn to continue: they knew that now they were to hear his final verdict.

'Man,' said the king of the Djinn in a solemn voice, 'is superior to all other animals because it is he and he alone who has been promised by the Maker a life after death. This life after death in this world may be in the gardens of Paradise or in the fires of Hell; it is for him to choose how he lives his present life on this earth. The animals, on the other hand, have only this one life on earth and have been granted no future life after death. How greatly, therefore, has the Almighty favoured man over animals by promising him everlasting life! For this reason man must be regarded as superior to all animals and is therefore their master. This is our verdict.'

At these words all the men clapped and cheered, while some of them stamped their feet as a sign of joy at their victory over the animals. As for the animals, they hung their heads in silence, for now they knew that the men had been declared their masters and that they must therefore accept being their slaves.

Once again, though, the king of the Djinn had not completed all he had to say. He was still standing in front of the men and animals as he waited for the cheering to die down. Then, raising his voice, he continued to address the assembly of men and animals.

'But let man not imagine,' he said, 'that just because he is superior to the animals they are his slaves. Rather it is that we are all slaves of the Almighty and must obey His commands. Man must know that, while he has rights over animals, he also has responsibilities towards them. He must know that he is master of them only because the Creator has appointed man as His representative on earth. Let man not forget that he is accountable to his Maker for the way in which he treats all animals, just as he is accountable for his behaviour towards his fellow human beings. Man bears a heavy responsibility, for we know that the Almighty will, on the Day of Judgement, hold him accountable for all his actions.

'And let us all remember that in the life of our beloved Prophet, may the blessings and peace of Allah be upon him, there are numerous stories that tell of his kindness to animals. Let us also remember that many of the Prophet's Sayings remind man of his duties towards animals: to help them in their lives and not to harm them, to give them food when they are hungry and water when they are thirsty, not to overwork them when they are tired and to be considerate to them in every way. So return home, all of you, in peace under the protection of Almighty Allah.'

And the animals and men walked out in thoughtful silence from the court of the king of the Djinn.

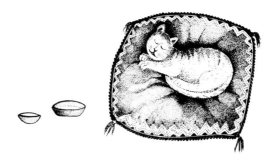